Mistress Scatterbrain, the Knight's Daughter

By Stéphane Daniel

Illustrated by Christophe Besse

Meet the Scatterbrains

Vivian Scatterbrain

Tom Scatterbrain

Queen Rose

CHAPTER 1
A Birthday Wish

Vivian Scatterbrain was playing a sad song on her lute. It was her birthday, but she was unhappy. Princesses were supposed to marry knights but she loved a squire called Edmund.

She had to delay getting married until Edmund could become a knight, so she came up with a plan. She met her parents, Tom and Rose Scatterbrain, downstairs. "My dear daughter," said her father, "you're a young woman now. It's time to get married. You'll need to get yourself kidnapped first so that a knight will come and rescue you."

"But how do I get kidnapped?"
asked Vivian.

"It's easy. Just find a dangerous place
and wait!" her father told her.

"I'm not sure I want to be kidnapped,"
said Vivian. "Can I choose the knight
myself? I could come up with some trials."

"That's not a bad idea," her mother said.

"All right," Tom Scatterbrain agreed.
"Let's arrange a few trials. But you will
have to marry the winner – even if it's the
Black Prince." The Black Prince was the
scariest knight in the kingdom.
"I believe in my lucky star," said Vivian
in hope.

CHAPTER 2
Pigeon Mail

Heading back to her bedroom, Vivian couldn't stop thinking of her beloved Edmund. Edmund's master was the Black Prince. He would never allow Edmund to become a knight.

Vivian knew that if her plan worked, the winner of the trials would refuse to marry her! She sat at her desk, took out her quill and wrote a letter:

My dear knights,

I have decided to marry the brave young man

that fate will bring me at Luckless Castle.

I believe that beneath the armour will stand a

most noble knight, who will also have the best

of squires. Marriage will be the reward for

whoever holds this parchment at the end of

the trials. If the winner should refuse to marry

me, I will respect that choice.

Vivian Scatterbrain

After writing the letter, Vivian went to sit by the window. She looked out, waiting for her pigeon, Scatterbeak, to bring her news from her beloved. Meanwhile, Sir Scatterbrain had selected four knights to compete for Vivian's hand in marriage. The big tournament was to be held the next day.

Vivian kept herself locked in her bedroom. She didn't even want to know the contestants' names.

The sound of flapping wings startled her and she looked up. A pigeon had landed on the window ledge.

Vivian let out a cry of joy. "Scatterbeak! At last!" She carefully took the piece of parchment attached to Scatterbeak's leg and read it:

Dearest Vivian,

I have nothing but fear for you, my darling.

The Black Prince went to see each of his competitors

in the tournament. He scared them all to make

them drop out. He will be the only one to take

part. Our fate is sealed. My sorrow is immense!

Edmund

Vivian immediately sat down to write

a reply:

My dear Edmund,

Please do not worry. The Black Prince can't

possibly win. Trust me. You are the one I love

and the one I will marry.

Vivian

Suddenly, just as she was about to give Scatterbeak her letter, there was a knock on the door.

To Vivian's surprise, her father entered the room carrying two baskets full of shopping.

"Your mother sent me to the village for groceries," he explained. "Have you decided on the trials yet?"

"Yes," replied Vivian. "I have planned two trials. For the first, the knights must stay seated on Moody Hooves for a walk around the courtyard."

"Good luck to them!" said her father. "Only you can ride that crazy horse of yours!"

"And for the second test," Vivian continued, "they will have to play me a tune on the lute."

"How unusual!" said Tom Scatterbrain.

"If the trials end in a draw," said Vivian, "there will be a final test. I have written a note on parchment, promising to marry the winner. The parchment will be hidden deep in Deadwood Forest. It will be in the dragon's lair, where my brother, Lancelot, once defeated the dragon. The knights will have to find it and bring it back."

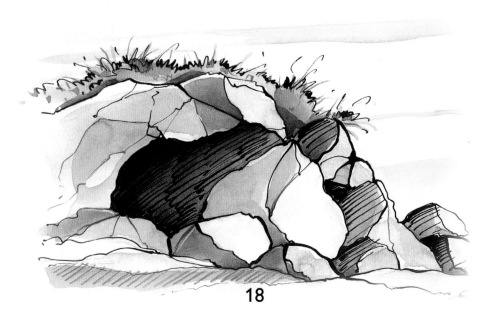

Vivian had one more idea.

"One last thing, Father. I want the knights to fight with their visors down. A knight's looks are not as important as his heart."

Tom Scatterbrain nodded, then picked up the baskets and started to walk away.

"Wait! What about the parchment?" Vivian remembered. "Someone needs to hide it!"

"I'll take care of that," said her father. Then Tom Scatterbrain stepped towards the door, but Vivian called him back.

"Haven't you forgotten this?" she said, handing her father the parchment. Tom Scatterbrain carefully slipped the parchment inside his shirt.

As soon as her father had left, Vivian

attached her love letter to Scatterbeak's leg,

kissed him on the head and sent him away.

"Go, Scatterbeak!" she cried. "Let my

beloved Edmund know that he has nothing

to worry about."

CHAPTER 3
The Trials Begin

In the castle courtyard, Sir Scatterbrain and Queen Rose were waiting for the knights to arrive. "Let the brave knights enter!" Tom Scatterbrain ordered.

Much to everyone's surprise, there were just two figures: a tall man in black armour, followed by his squire.

"I am the Black Prince," said the knight.

"I don't think it will take long to find a knight to marry your daughter."

Tom Scatterbrain looked confused. "But where are the other knights?" he said, turning to Queen Rose.

"They were all too busy," said the Black Prince. "You can declare me the winner. Now, where is the beautiful princess?"

"Wait!" called the voice of another knight,

marching through the castle gates.

"Who are you?"
the Black Prince
asked him.

"My name is the White

Prince and I would like to

challenge you," the

knight in white replied.

"Well, in that case," Tom Scatterbrain announced, "let the trials begin! The first task is to ride this horse around the courtyard. Good luck!"

"I'll go first," the White Prince said quickly. The White Prince mounted the horse and easily completed the ride, then dismounted.

"Is that it?" asked the Black Prince in surprise. "That's too easy!" he chuckled. As soon as the Black Prince mounted the horse, it kicked its back legs in the air and sent the Black Prince flying!

Sir Scatterbrain declared the White Prince

the winner of the first trial. The Black Prince

sat on the ground, dazed.

Edmund rushed to help his master. He was

not used to seeing the Black Prince defeated.

Edmund was puzzled as he watched the White Prince walk away. He gazed up at Vivian's window, but she was nowhere to be seen.

Meanwhile, the White Prince sat in the
kitchen and lifted up her helmet visor.
No one knew that underneath the armour
it was really Vivian!

Her plan was working. She just had one trial
left to win. Then, as the White Prince, she
could reject the marriage. Edmund would
have time to become a knight and they
could finally be together.

A drum roll echoed through the castle. Vivian put her helmet back on and became the White Prince again.

"Gentlemen," Tom Scatterbrain began. "I'm afraid that I can't remember what my daughter said, so I thought she might like to see some wrestling. Whoever falls outside the circle is the loser."

"Excuse me!" the White Prince interrupted "Would Princess Vivian really enjoy wrestling? Are you sure that you can't remember what she really wanted?"

"No I can't, but Scatterbrains always know how to improvise," he replied with pride.

A few seconds later, the Black Prince let out a terrifying roar and launched himself at the White Prince. Immediately, the White Prince stepped back, out of the circle. There was no way Vivian could win.

"The Black Prince has won the second trial!" Tom Scatterbrain announced. "As it's a draw, there will be a third trial to find the winner. Bring your horses to the castle gates. You must go to the forest and bring back the message that has been hidden in a cave. Good luck!"

CHAPTER 4
The Hidden Parchment

The two contenders were off in a flash. When they approached the forest, they went in separate directions. The White Prince soon reached the dragon's lair. She knew the location very well as her father had brought her there before.

She found the parchment and opened it.

4 large leeks

Chicken legs

A loaf of bread

Straw wine

Oh dear! This was her mum's shopping list! Her dad had clearly mixed up the two parchments. Without her message to the winner, her plan was not going to work.

"What a disaster!" thought Vivian. She had made a terrible mistake! She had attached the wrong parchment to Scatterbeak's leg. Now she would have to marry the Black Prince! The White Prince rushed back to the castle. The Black Prince was already waiting there when Vivian returned. He looked equally empty-handed.

"Who has found the parchment?" Tom Scatterbrain asked. Above their heads, a bird was frantically flapping its wings.  Scatterbeak flew in circles, as if looking for something, then he decided to plunge towards the Black Prince and landed on his arm.

"What is wrong with Scatterbeak?" the White Prince wondered. The Black Prince unfolded the parchment that he noticed attached to the bird's leg.

"What's that, Black Prince?" Tom Scatterbrain asked him.

"I believe that I may have found the parchment we were looking for," said the Black Prince as he began to read it out:

My dear knights,

I have decided to marry the brave young

man that fate...

CHAPTER 5
The Truth Revealed

All of a sudden, the loud cries of a man

shouting echoed round the courtyard:

"Stop! Everyone stop!"

What a sight! The man wore patchy trousers, a dirty undershirt and had crazy, wild hair. He ran in bare feet towards the two knights, shouting: "I should be the one to marry the princess!"

"Who are you?" Queen Rose asked him.

"I'm the real Black Prince," he replied.

"So who is this Black Prince?" the queen said, pointing to the knight in black armour.

Silently, the Black Prince took off his helmet. It was Edmund! Vivian's heart skipped a beat!

"This traitor tied me up in the forest while we were looking for the parchment and stole my armour!" the Black Prince raged. Queen Rose ignored him and spoke to Edmund: "You, sir, have completed the trials so you are the winner. Please read the parchment." The Black Prince was furious. He grabbed a corner of the parchment and pulled so hard it tore in two. But it was too late, he had already lost.

 The Black Prince looked stunned, while the White Prince hurried out of the courtyard.

A few moments later, Vivian rushed up to her parents. "So, who am I to marry?" she asked, out of breath.

"Me!" Edmund smiled, delighted.

The Black Prince was still furious.

"Edmund can't marry a princess –

he doesn't fight. He

doesn't own a castle!

And he's not even

a knight!"

"I can change that," Tom Scatterbrain replied. He took his sword out of its scabbard and asked Edmund to kneel down. Then he tapped his sword three times on Edmund's shoulders.

"Now you really are a knight,"
he told Edmund. "It's time
to start celebrating
the wedding!"
With all hope lost, the
Black Prince left the castle.
"I knew I should trust
my lucky star!" Vivian laughed. Edmund
smiled and took her in his arms.

Franklin Watts
First published in Great Britain in 2015 by
The Watts Publishing Group

© RAGEOT-EDITEUR Paris, 2010
First published in French as
La Fille Du Chevalier Têtenlère

Translation © Franklin Watts 2015
English text and adaptation by Fabrice
Blanchefort.

Series Editor: Melanie Palmer
Series Advisor: Catherine Glavina
Cover Designer: Cathryn Gilbert
Design Manager: Peter Scoulding

ISBN 978 1 4451 3726 1 (hbk)
ISBN 978 1 4451 3729 2 (pbk)
ISBN 978 1 4451 3727 8 (ebook)
ISBN 978 1 4451 3728 5 (library ebook)

Printed in China

Franklin Watts
An imprint of
Hachette Children's Group
Part of The Watts Publishing Group
Carmelite House
50 Victoria Embankment
London EC4Y 0DZ

An Hachette UK Company
www.hachette.co.uk

www.franklinwatts.co.uk